Acting Edition

72 Miles To Go...

by Hilary Bettis

I0591882

FOR PRODUCTION INQUIRIES

UNITED STATES AND CANADA
info@concordtheatricals.com
1-866-979-0447

UNITED KINGDOM AND EUROPE
licensing@concordtheatricals.co.uk
020-7054-7298

Each title is subject to availability from Concord Theatricals Corp., depending upon country of performance. Please be aware that *72 MILES TO GO...* may not be licensed by Concord Theatricals Corp. in your territory. Professional and amateur producers should contact the nearest Concord Theatricals Corp. office or licensing partner to verify availability.

MUSIC AND THIRD-PARTY MATERIALS USE NOTE

IMPORTANT BILLING AND CREDIT REQUIREMENTS

72 MILES TO GO... was originally produced in New York City by Roundabout Theatre Company at the Harold and Miriam Steinberg Center for Theatre/Laura Pels Theatre on March 10, 2020. The production was directed by Jo Bonney, with set design by Rachel Hauck, costume design by Emilio Sosa, lighting design by Lap Chi Chu, and sound design by Elisheba Ittoop. The production stage manager was Donald Fried. The cast was as follows:

BILLY	Triney Sandoval
ANITA	Maria Elena Ramirez
CHRISTIAN	Bobby Moreno
EVA	Jacqueline Guillén
AARON	Tyler Alvarez

72 MILES TO GO... received a workshop at the Alley Theatre (James Black, Interim Artistic Director; Dean R. Gladden, Managing Director). It was directed by José Zayas, with scenic and lighting design by Kevin Rigdon, costume design by Haydee Zelideth, and sound design by Megumi Katayama. The stage manager was Rebecca R.D. Hamlin. The cast was as follows:

BILLY	Orlando Arriaga
ANITA	Briana J. Resa
CHRISTIAN	Christopher Salazar
EVA	Melissa Molano
AARON	Juan Sebastian Cruz

72 MILES TO GO... was developed in part with the support of the Crossing Borders (Cruzando Fronteras) Festival at Two River Theater, in Red Bank, New Jersey.

72 MILES TO GO... received its first professional reading as part of PlayFest at Orlando Shakes in partnership with UCF in 2018.

CHARACTERS

BILLY – (47-55) Chicano, pastor at a Unitarian church
ANITA – (42-50) Mexican, living in Nogales, Mexico
CHRISTIAN – (23-31) Chicano, dreams of being a Marine
EVA – (17-25) Chicana, the caretaker
AARON – (14-22) Chicano, loves science

SETTING

Tucson, Arizona

TIME

The play spans eight years, from 2008-2016

AUTHOR'S NOTES

Punctuation

A slash (/) is an interruption.
An ellipsis (...) indicates thoughts trailing off.
A *(Pause.)* direction indicates a three-to-five-second beat.
A *(Silence.)* direction lasts for fifteen to twenty seconds, long and uncomfortable, often because no one knows what to say.

Production Notes

We only hear Anita's voice. This shouldn't be exaggerated in any way. No images, no projections, no actors onstage, no God mic. Just her voice coming from the actual phone. Almost as though she is a ghost...

Like a piece of music, this play only works when the rhythm is played. If it's too slow, it loses its emotional engine. If it's too fast, it loses its meaning. Please don't add pauses where there aren't any. Please don't rush over the silences and pauses.

Life should never stop onstage. Time rushes by in the transitions. We see them living. Waiting by the phone, a new baby, moving out.

ACKNOWLEDGEMENTS

This play would not exist without all these incredible people.

Thank you to the entire staff at Roundabout, who were beyond generous and encouraging despite the looming global pandemic that would close this show forty-eight hours after it opened. I'm especially grateful to Todd Haimes, whose belief in this play made it part of his incredible legacy, and my brilliant friend, Jill Rafson, whose fierce support for playwrights is invaluable. Thank you to the talented cast and designers who brought this story to life in ways I could have never imagined. And last, a big thank you to Jo Bonney for her tireless leadership, guiding us through all the ups and downs of production with unwavering dedication.

This play started in 2017 at WildWind Lab at Texas Tech. I showed up with a cast and no script, and left with the first sixty pages five days later. Thank you, Michael, for not freaking out when I showed up with nothing but a blank page. And thank you to my dramaturg, Rachel Lerner-Ley, who spent days with me in that tiny dorm room, mapping the timeline of our country's nebulous immigration policy.

I have to thank The Alley Theatre, my home away from home, who gave this play both a workshop production in 2019 and a full production in 2021. I want to express my deepest gratitude to Rob Melrose and Liz Frankel, who have believed in every draft of just about everything I write. Thank you to Lily Wolff, who's always one of the smartest people in the room. And a special thank you to my second husband, José Zayas, for making me better, talking me off the cliff, and inspiring me to keep going.

Thank you to John Dias and Stephanie Coen at Two River Theater for giving this play space at Crossing Borders and nominating it for the Blackburn Prize, which meant so much to me. And to Jim Helsinger, Cynthia White, and Kristin Clippard at Orlando Shakes for giving me a week in sunny Florida to develop this script.

A special thank you is owed to Geoffrey Hoffman, who serves as both a law professor at the University of Houston and an immigration judge. His invaluable contributions to this play cannot be overstated, as he meticulously fact-checked multiple drafts, ensuring accuracy and authenticity in its portrayal of our complex immigration system. His expertise and insights have been instrumental in shedding light on the realities and challenges that these families endure.

I have to thank the love of my life, Bobby Moreno, for reading every word of everything, and believing in me when I need it most.

Above all, my deepest gratitude belongs to the undocumented families who live this reality. Thank you for being the backbone of this country. You matter. You're as American as it gets. You are worthy of safety, compassion, and dignity. May our laws catch up to our souls.

"La esperanza le pertenece a la vida, es la vida misma defendiéndose." – Julio Cortázar

"Hope belongs to life, it's life itself defending itself."

Prologue

(Church music plays.* Maybe a chorus of voices singing, maybe not.)

*(A man in a minister's robe, **BILLY**, walks out to the onstage pulpit.)*

(He listens to the music as though it's the most beautiful thing he's ever heard.)

(The music comes to an end.)

BILLY. Hallelujah and amen.

(He scans the crowd.)

I don't think I've seen the room this full in my thirty years preaching here. Y'all really that excited to see me go?

(Beat as he waits for a response...)

That was my attempt at a joke. There's a reason the Good Lord made me a preacher and not a comedian.

(Beat as he waits for a response...)

I keep throwing them out, but they don't seem to land Well, folks, ever since I announced my retirement, I started working on the sermon for my final Sunday. I've had two months to really prepare and practice. I wrote

---

*A license to produce *72 Miles To Go...* does not include a performance license for any third-party or copyrighted music. Licensees should create an original composition or use music in the public domain. For further information, please see the Music and Third-Party Materials Use Note on page iii.

at least a dozen versions, then finally settled on one. I practiced on my kids until they stopped talking to me. I practiced on my wife until she threatened divorce.

Y'all are tough. We go way back, and you're still this tough on me?

I spent months and months working on this sermon, trying to get every word just right. Hoping to leave this congregation I love so deeply with some words that'll stick with you after I'm gone...

But I'm standing here now, and none of these words feel right. So I hope y'all will forgive me for going off the cuff.

(He tears up his sermon.)

That was a bit dramatic, but I couldn't resist the theatrics of it.

I woke up this morning filled with a lot of doubt. You ever have those days?

(He scans the audience.)

So I closed my eyes, flipped open my Bible, and landed on Matthew 5:12. "Rejoice and be glad, for your reward is great in Heaven..."

"Rejoice and be glad, for your reward is great in Heaven..." What does that mean?

Now, I've been up front with y'all over the years that I have my doubts about a literal Heaven. And since you keep coming back, I figure a lot of you in this room have your doubts, too.

"Rejoice and be glad, for your reward is great in Heaven..."

(Beat as he lets the audience digest that.)

The older I get, the more I realize that a lifetime is just bits and pieces of memory.

Like the first time I stepped on this pulpit, filled with arrogance and youth, thinking I could change the world.

The sound of my kids racing to the TV to watch Saturday morning cartoons.

Or the first time I saw my wife...

(He drifts off. Remembering.)

Through the years, I've gone back to that memory over and over, picking it apart. Wondering if way deep down a part of me knew I was staring at my future.

But the truth is, I could've gone a million different directions. And she could've gone a million different directions.

I've had folks ask me over the years – lawyers and friends and neighbors and my dear friend, Officer Garcia, who's here with us today – "If you knew then what you know now, would you still have fallen in love?"

A silly question, isn't it?

One

(August. 2008.)

(The kitchen.)

(Early morning light. The radio quietly plays some top-forties pop song.)*

*(**EVA** slowly puts on blue eye shadow, but she's clearly distracted. Something on her mind.)*

*(**AARON**, still in his pajamas, pokes his head in the door.)*

AARON. Eva...

(She startles.)

EVA. You gave me a heart attack.

AARON. Christian isn't in his bed.

EVA. *(Trying to reassure him).* I bet he stayed at Angela's last night.

AARON. But what if he didn't? What if he got stopped?

EVA. He's okay. You're gonna give yourself another ulcer. Take a deep breath.

*(**AARON** does.)*

Why are you up so early? I'll wake you up in an hour. Want me to make chocolate-chip pancakes with whip cream?

AARON. And bacon.

EVA. Okay, I'll make / bacon.

AARON. What if no one at school likes me?

EVA. Everyone likes you. Plus you'll have Steve and Diego.

AARON. We're not in any of the same classes.

EVA. You have me and if anyone says anything to you I'll mess them up.

AARON. Promise?

EVA. I promise. Go back to bed.

AARON. *(One breath.)* I can't sleep. I dreamed there was this huge flood and it poured into our house and no one could swim except me, but I couldn't hold you and Dad and Mom, and Christian, and then we all drown / and –

EVA. Shhh... Feel my face.

>   *(***AARON*** *does.)*

AARON. What if people ask about Mom?

>   *(Pause.)*

EVA. Just say she's away on business.

AARON. When is she coming home?

EVA. I don't know, baby.

>   *(***BILLY*** *enters.)*

BILLY. So much for me beating the two of you up. I was gonna surprise you with breakfast.

AARON. Eva's gonna make pancakes and bacon.

BILLY. I can do / that.

AARON. But you have to make it with chocolate chips and whip cream like Mom does.

EVA. Just let me make it Dad.

BILLY. Am I really that bad?

EVA. You burn everything.

AARON. Or it's tuna and noodles.

BILLY. That's a staple.

AARON. Christian didn't /

BILLY. Hey, what do you call a fake noodle? An impasta /

AARON. Christian didn't come home.

EVA. He probably stayed at Angela's.

> (**BILLY** *takes a deep breath.*)

BILLY. He's a grown man. I know you want to protect him, but we gotta let him live his life.

AARON. I know, but he speeds and he shouldn't even be driving!

BILLY. Well I'll have a talk with him about that / okay?

AARON. He shouldn't / Dad.

BILLY. What are you most excited about?

AARON. Biology. You get to dissect frogs, which I didn't want to at first, but Steve said they just put them to sleep nicely and he said it's the only way to be a veterinarian. So I guess that.

> (**CHRISTIAN**, *holding a dozen donuts, saunters in.*)

> (**AARON** *lunges at him.*)

You have to call if you don't come home! FUCKING ASSHOLE!

BILLY.	EVA.
Hey, hey, language!	Aaron!

CHRISTIAN. Whoa, okay, dude. Relax. I brought you donuts.

AARON. I don't want your stupid donuts.

CHRISTIAN. Fine. More yummy delicious donuts for me.

AARON. I thought you were / gone.

CHRISTIAN. I'm standing right here, Lil' Homie.

BILLY. I'll eat one. You got a bear claw in there?

CHRISTIAN. *(Defensive.)* I brought them for Eva / and Aaron.

EVA. I don't want mine, / so you can have it, Dad.

BILLY. A dozen donuts?

CHRISTIAN. And?

> *(They stare each other down.)*

BILLY. Alright. I'll make pancakes.

CHRISTIAN. I try to do something nice, but fine.

EVA. Okay, you guys do not get to be assholes on MY first day of senior year. If you wanna be dicks go outside so I don't have to listen to it!

> *(Ringing. Everyone rushes to the phone like the world is on fire.)*

BILLY. Hi, baby. No, no, everyone's up. I'll put you on speaker.

> *(**ANITA** is on the other end. We only hear her, and watch the way the family holds the phone, as though it is human.)*

ANITA. *(Exhausted, but trying to hide it.)* Hi, babies.

ALL KIDS. Hi, Mom.

BILLY. *(Concern.)* Where are you?

ANITA. At the soup kitchen. I only have a minute. Conejito, what are you wearing to school?

AARON. Dirty clothes because Eva didn't do laundry /

EVA. Stop lying! I washed his clothes.

ANITA. Eva, don't wear too much makeup. That blue eye shadow makes you look cheap. Mi Rey. How are you adjusting to being home?

CHRISTIAN. I'm okay.

ANITA. I know things are hard between you and Billy, but try to be kind to each other.

AARON. He's hanging out with Angela again. Staying out ALL night and DRIVING /

CHRISTIAN. Hey! You trying to get me in / trouble?

ANITA. Don't get her pregnant.

CHRISTIAN. We're careful.

ANITA. Yes, but sometimes things happen. And... I don't... I don't want you to ever go through *this*, mi Rey.

> *(Beat, then back to business.)*

I spoke with Mr. Gomez last night. He says I can apply for a request for re-entry. If they approve it, I can apply for humanitarian parole. Then I can come home for Eva's graduation.

EVA. If they don't?

ANITA. They will. I am not missing your graduation.

BILLY. I'll call him today and see what we need to do.

ANITA. It costs a lot of money. I'm looking for a job.

BILLY. We'll figure it out, sweetheart.

ANITA. I hate being such a burden.

BILLY. You're not a burden.

ANITA. Send lots of pictures, babies. I want to see everything! Are you taking the bus?

EVA. Eddie's picking / us up.

AARON. They tongue / kiss!

EVA. We don't / tongue kiss!

AARON. Yes you do. I've seen them tongue / kiss.

CHRISTIAN. Mom, Eva's tongue / kissing!

BILLY. I'll get the shotgun / loaded.

EVA. We don't even have a shotgun!

BILLY. I better go buy one.

EVA. Stop! I love him!

ANITA. Make sure you shoot him right between the eyes, Billy.

> *(They laugh.)*

AARON. Mom? Can we come see you?

ANITA. *(Stern.)* No, baby. Not here. Not like this. I have to go.

> *(Beat.)*

El amor no tiene fronteras...bye babies.

> *(**ANITA** hangs up. Click.)*
>
> *(Silence as they stare at the phone... It's too much.)*

BILLY. Aaron, go get in the shower.

> *(**AARON** leaves.)*

>   (**CHRISTIAN** *starts to follow him.*)

EVA. Dad /

BILLY. Christian, hold on a minute /

EVA. I'm almost eighteen, and it's my senior year. I need my license.

BILLY. *(Dry.)* Cars are deadly weapons. Do you want to fly through the windshield and die?

EVA. Fine.

>   *(Rage.)*

You should have called you fucking asshole.

>   *(She leaves.)*

BILLY. We're very happy you're home, but as long as you live under my roof, you live by this family's rules. We have a plan in place. You always call. Always. That is non-negotiable.

CHRISTIAN. I'm not a teenager.

BILLY. The kids need you. Last time she was deported it almost killed them – especially Aaron.

CHRISTIAN. Yeah, well, it wasn't exactly fun for me /

BILLY. You weren't here! You decide to run away without telling anyone /

CHRISTIAN. Whose fault is that, *Billy*?

BILLY. You wanna take your anger out on me, go ahead, but not in front of them.

CHRISTIAN. Don't worry, I won't be here long.

>   (**CHRISTIAN** *starts to leave.*)

BILLY. Hey.

CHRISTIAN. What now?

BILLY. Don't speed.

Two

(November. 2008.)

(The kitchen.)

*(**BILLY** is working on his sermon.)*

*(**CHRISTIAN** enters. He goes to the fridge and gets a beer, but he doesn't open it. He stands there, staring at the bottle...)*

BILLY. Something on your mind?

CHRISTIAN. No...

*(**BILLY** goes back to his writing.)*

*(A moment as **CHRISTIAN** stares at the bottle.)*

BILLY. Seems like something's bothering you.

CHRISTIAN. I don't know. I went to six restaurants, no one's hiring without papers. And then I stood outside Home Depot for five hours.

(Sarcastic.) An old lady hit on me. Some kid offered to pay me in tacos if I cleaned his bedroom...

BILLY. *(Trying to make a joke.)* Sounds like a good deal. You'll find something.

CHRISTIAN. I've been looking for three months.

BILLY. You gonna drink that beer?

CHRISTIAN. I don't know. It sounded good, and now it doesn't.

BILLY. I could use one.

*(**CHRISTIAN** pulls a beer from the fridge, hands it to **BILLY**.)*

I'm stuck. Writer's block. Sometimes I just don't have anything inspiring to say, but people come no matter. Maybe if I read it out loud I'll find my way over the hump. Want to hear /

CHRISTIAN. Not / really.

BILLY. I won't bore you with all of it, just this paragraph I'm stuck on.

(Reading from his pad.) "I'll be the first to admit forgiveness is a lofty ideal. Yet it's something we all crave, something we all want deep down, because not one of us walking this planet hasn't sinned. Colossians 3:13 says, 'Bear with each other and forgive one another if any of you has a grievance / against someone. Forgive as the Lord forgave you.'"

CHRISTIAN. Boring.

BILLY. Well... That's where I get stuck anyway. Any thoughts?

CHRISTIAN. I'm not the brains of the family. You should ask Eva.

BILLY. *(Making a joke.)* She usually just corrects my English, my grammar...

CHRISTIAN. *(Smiling.)* Yeah... The letters I sent her from Iowa, she'd send them back with red pen marks. Where does a skill like that get you in life?

BILLY. She'll probably be some politician or famous journalist.

CHRISTIAN. Must be nice to have options.

BILLY. Don't be bitter at your sister for something neither of you have / control over.

CHRISTIAN. Dude, don't.

*(**BILLY** goes back to his writing.)*

(**CHRISTIAN** *cracks open his beer. Drinks.*)

Angela wants to get married.

BILLY. Do you?

CHRISTIAN. I mean, we've been together since high school. She waited for me while I was in Iowa. Only cheated on me a few times, but that's fine because I cheated on her, so we figured it was even. I love her. She's my soulmate, I know that.

(*Proud.*) I don't really even want to fuck other girls.

BILLY. That's a good sign.

CHRISTIAN. Yeah.

BILLY. Rings are expensive.

CHRISTIAN. Angela doesn't care about that.

BILLY. So what's the problem?

CHRISTIAN. I can't get married if Mom isn't there.

(**BILLY** *digests this.*)

BILLY. Does Angela know how you feel?

CHRISTIAN. She says she can't put her life on hold forever. I tell her it's not forever. Mom will get re-entry for Eva's graduation. We could have the wedding then – It's not even just Mom. I'm a ticking bomb /

BILLY. You don't know that /

CHRISTIAN. Turn on the news, Billy. Arpaio's launching a state-wide hunt like we're pests in need of extermination. Two guys from Home Depot climbed in a truck last week and never / came back.

BILLY. If you ever suspect something's off, you go straight to the church and you call me.

CHRISTIAN. (*Oozing sarcasm.*) Wow, that's good advice.

(Silence.)

BILLY. Marry Angela. Your mom'll be there.

CHRISTIAN. *(Hopeful.)* She got her re-entry?

BILLY. No. Her request was denied.

CHRISTIAN. Okay so how's she...

(It hits him.)

She's not crossing the desert again. There's legal ways /

BILLY. We've exhausted everything.

CHRISTIAN. Then we'll wait.

BILLY. I'm not waiting forever to share a bed with my wife!

CHRISTIAN. You have to! If we get Mom here the right way, we can stop living like fugitives. I can stop living like a fugitive.

(Vulnerable.) Please, Billy.

BILLY. Christian...

CHRISTIAN. If Mom keeps crossing illegally, if you help her, they'll assume I'm the same. You wanna give them an excuse to deport me too? Oh, wait, I forgot who I'm talking to – you'll probably invite ICE to my wedding /

BILLY. That's an ugly thing to / say.

CHRISTIAN. I thought I'd be in the Marines with my own house by now! But, yeah, shit on more dreams /

BILLY. I was trying to protect you.

CHRISTIAN. Is lying to a kid about his citizenship in the Bible somewhere?

BILLY. I've spent a lifetime – and every penny I have – trying to get this family legal.

CHRISTIAN. Must have been hard for you.

BILLY. I thought the laws would change. Why break my kid's heart if I didn't need to?

CHRISTIAN. Until you fucking did!

BILLY. It's been five years. I'm not doing this.

CHRISTIAN. You gave me USMC gear for Christmas / every year!

BILLY. Because you asked / for it.

CHRISTIAN. You watched *Platoon* and *Apocalypse Now* and *Saving Private Ryan* with me, and told me what a / great soldier I'd be!

BILLY. Christian /

CHRISTIAN. We sang the Marine Corp Hymn /

BILLY. It's a good song /

CHRISTIAN. You drove me to the recruiter's office – for my eighteenth birthday! What was your plan? Make me a fake birth certificate?

BILLY. Yeah. I thought about it.

CHRISTIAN. You knew I could have been deported, and you still drove me /

BILLY. Well you weren't! I told you the truth before you walked in /

CHRISTIAN. I could forgive you for all of that. But what I can't forgive is that for eighteen years you LIED about being MY DAD. You're a coward /

BILLY. Okay /

CHRISTIAN. I'm glad you're not my father /

BILLY. Okay /

CHRISTIAN. I'm glad I don't have a coward's blood /

BILLY. Okay /

CHRISTIAN. Maybe me and Mom would have been better off if you left us in the desert to die /

BILLY. *(Explodes.)* THAT'S ENOUGH!

> *(Silence.)*

(Vulnerable.) Not for a moment, do I regret marrying your mom and raising you as my... Not for a moment.

> *(The sound of a car outside.* **BILLY** *pulls himself together.)*

Kids are home.

CHRISTIAN. Billy.

BILLY. What?

CHRISTIAN. *(Pleading.)* Look at me and promise me you won't risk my life.

> **(BILLY** *looks at* **CHRISTIAN.** *He swallows. He nods.)*

BILLY. I promise.

> **(AARON** *and* **EVA** *barge through the door.* **AARON** *crudely mimes making out.)*

EVA. Stop it!

BILLY. Oh, was that Eddie driving / you home?

EVA. Yep.

BILLY. How come he never comes in?

EVA. Because he's the love of my life and I don't want you to shoot him.

BILLY. Why? Is there a reason? Did he mouth-kiss / you?

AARON. All they do is "mouth-kiss" /

BILLY. How was your day / buddy?

AARON. I got an A on my biology / test!

BILLY. That's / great.

AARON. Mr. Hopkins says if I keep it up, I could take advanced biology / next year!

EVA. I'm making Frito pie for dinner to celebrate. Don't tell / Mom.

AARON. Don't put any meat in it.

EVA. Why?!

BILLY. Meat's the best part!

AARON. *(Proud.)* I'm a vegetarian now /

EVA. Since when?

AARON. Homeroom. Luis Sanchez has an iPhone 3G, and he showed me a slaughterhouse video! It was horrible!

>   (**CHRISTIAN** *guzzles his beer, storms out.*)

Where are you going?

CHRISTIAN. Nowhere.

>   (**CHRISTIAN** *leaves.*)

Three

(April. 2009.)

(A truck.)

*(**BILLY** drives.)*

*(**EVA**, in a prom dress, sits in the passenger seat, quietly crying.)*

*(Music plays on the radio. Some twangy country song that **BILLY** sings along to. Maybe a song in the style of "All My Exes Live In Texas."*)*

*(**EVA** listens until she can't stand it any longer. This goes on for an excruciatingly long time. She turns the radio off.)*

EVA. Can you just...

(Awkward silence.)

*(**BILLY** pulls out a candy.)*

BILLY. Ginger candy?

EVA. *(Petulant.)* I don't like ginger.

BILLY. What? Since when?

EVA. I don't know. Twelve.

---

*A license to produce *72 Miles To Go...* does not include a performance license for "All My Exes Live In Texas." The publisher and author suggest that the licensee contact ASCAP or BMI to ascertain the music publisher and contact such music publisher to license or acquire permission for performance of the song. If a license or permission is unattainable for "All My Exes Live In Texas," the licensee may not use the song in *72 Miles To Go...* but should create an original composition in a similar style, or use a similar song in the public domain. For further information, please see the Music and Third-Party Materials Use Note on page iii.

BILLY. Alright, well, it's got your name on it if you change your mind.

> *(Pause.)*

You might want it for your breath.

EVA. Why?

BILLY. Well, I can smell the beer. I mean, at least pretend like you don't want your dad to know you're drunk.

> (**EVA** *makes a show of putting the candy in her mouth.*)

So...anything you wanna talk about /

EVA. Not really.

BILLY. Okay.

> *(Pause.)*

We're Unitarian, so...

> *(Pause.)*

Prrreeetty open-minded...

> *(Pause.)*

I drank at my prom. First time. I was trying to show off to Melinda Flores, so I drank a twelve-pack...puked all night.

> *(Pause.)*

Yeah...crawled home drunk. Hungover for days with that disgusting puke smell on my breath... The moral of the story is I never drank again.

EVA. You keep beer in the fridge. And it wasn't my first time drinking. And I didn't puke.

> *(Pause.)*

BILLY. Hey, did you see in the news they made round bails of hay illegal? Said it's because cows weren't getting a square meal.

(**EVA** *sobs. Vulnerable.*)

Peanut, I'm sorry. It was just a joke. Cows can eat whatever / they want.

EVA. I shouldn't have gone. I didn't need a dress or shoes or... We should have used that money for Mom's re-entry.

BILLY. Are you crazy? Your mom would have killed both of us if you didn't go to your / senior prom.

EVA. It was a waste! When is she coming home?

BILLY. I don't / know.

EVA. She promised she'd be home for my graduation! Don't you talk to the lawyer every day?

(Rage.) WHY DON'T YOU DO SOMETHING!

(Silence. Cries until she stops.)

BILLY. Did anything... I mean... You know, that whole prom-thing.

EVA. Prom-thing?

BILLY. You know, like...that movie Christian used to watch.

EVA. What movie?

BILLY. That prom movie. Pie something...about pie. Ruined pie for me, I'll tell you that.

EVA. *American Pie?*

BILLY. That's it. I knew it was about pie.

EVA. *(Pointed.)* Are you asking if I had SEX with Eddie?

BILLY. I... Just, you know, high school and...the whole indulging in foreplay situations.

EVA. What? I am not talking to you about this.

BILLY. Eddie looks like a frog, so...with his eyes. I always thought you could do better.

EVA. *(She's lying.)* I'm not stupid. It's not like I thought Eddie was the one.

BILLY. Good. I was getting nervous about having ugly grandchildren. I think we both dodged a bullet.

>   *(Pause.)*

You know, if you ever need to talk about that stuff...

EVA. Sex?

BILLY. That stuff, or other stuff... Birth control. If you ever need anything, you know... I mean, we're Unitarian, so... I'm a Unitarian pastor.

EVA. Okay.

BILLY. Jesus hung out with hookers. Anyone who tells you otherwise isn't reading the Bible properly.

EVA. Oh my God, you have to stop.

BILLY. I guess I just mean sex isn't *thaaat* big of a deal. Everyone does it. Animals /

EVA. Stop. I need my mom for this shit. Not you.

>   *(After a few moments, **BILLY** pulls over and turns the engine off.)*

Are you gonna murder me and leave me on the side of the road?

BILLY. I thought about it, but I changed my mind. How many beers you have?

EVA. I'm not drunk. I have self-control unlike you.

BILLY. Prove it. Arms out. Touch your nose.

(**EVA** *does* **BILLY***'s "sobriety" check. She passes.*)

You ready?

EVA. For?

BILLY. This truck isn't gonna drive itself home.

EVA. *(Skeptical.)* Really?

BILLY. Yep.

(*They switch places.*)

Alright, now adjust the mirrors /

(**EVA** *adjusts the mirrors, puts on the lights, starts the engine, and pulls out like a pro.*)

Oh. Well I guess you've got this.

EVA. *(Indignant.)* Driver's ed is mandatory junior year. Plus Mom used to let me drive when we went to Costco. It was sort of our thing.

BILLY. So I'm the one way behind the curve ball?

EVA. Eight ball, Dad. You want to be behind the curve ball.

BILLY. *(To himself.)* Eight ball... After Christian ran away, I just... And then losing your mom.

EVA. I'm not going anywhere.

BILLY. Well, you're going off to college. I need to get used to this. Not you.

EVA. I'm not going to college until Mom comes home.

BILLY. What?

EVA. Aaron needs me here until he graduates.

BILLY. He's not your responsibility.

EVA. He sleeps on the floor in my room. He sits with me at lunch.

BILLY. He'll be okay.

EVA. He gets picked on /

BILLY. You're going to college!

(**EVA** *slams on the brakes, startling* **BILLY**.)

EVA. I love you, but it's MY decision.

Four

(May. 2009.)

(The kitchen.)

*(**EVA**, in a nice dress, is in the middle of ironing Aaron's shirt, while simultaneously trying to cook and practice a speech.)*

*(**AARON** is preoccupied with something in a box.)*

*(**CHRISTIAN**, covered in dirt and wearing work boots, drinks a beer while doing a crossword puzzle.)*

(Everyone is in their own world.)

EVA. "Today, my friends, we find ourselves thinking only of the future, our dreams, the road ahead and the childhoods we are leaving / behind –"

CHRISTIAN. Are you gonna imagine everyone in the / auditorium naked?

EVA. "So I want to leave you all with a quote from William Shakespeare: 'It is not in the stars to hold our destiny but in ourselves.' Thank / you."

CHRISTIAN. And the naked crowd goes wild!

(He makes cheering sound effects.)

EVA. Aaron, go get in the / shower.

AARON. Two minutes /

EVA. Now /

AARON. Stop telling / me what to do!

EVA. Go!

CHRISTIAN. Listen / to your sister.

AARON. Hold on! I'm doing something important.

> (**CHRISTIAN** *lunges for the box.*)

AARON.	**CHRISTIAN**.
Don't!	What's in there?
	EVA.
Nothing!	Hey, guy /

EVA. Please go get ready before I have a nervous breakdown!

> (**CHRISTIAN** *lunges again, getting the box. He runs around the room as* **AARON** *chases him.* **EVA** *yells at them to stop. All three ad-lib.*)

AARON. Hey! Give it back! Give it back!

> (**CHRISTIAN** *looks inside.*)

CHRISTIAN. It's a turtle /

EVA. What?

CHRISTIAN. Did you know he had a / turtle?

AARON. Give her / back!

CHRISTIAN. Apparently it's a / girl.

EVA. Why do you have a turtle? We can't / afford pets.

AARON. Diego wanted to run her over with a lawn mower. I had no choice.

CHRISTIAN. He's got a point.

EVA. I thought Diego was a nice kid.

AARON. He was until he started hanging out with Cooper Michaels. I don't want to talk about it. Her name is Esmerelda. She only eats lettuce and bugs, which is practically free. Give her back!

> (**CHRISTIAN** *does.*)

EVA. You should've asked!

AARON. Who?

EVA. Me.

AARON. Yeah / okay.

EVA. I buy all the groceries, out of money I earn! I / work –

AARON. Okay! Sorry.

EVA. Can one of you please go get in the shower? / Please?

AARON. Are you making chicken?

EVA. Yes.

AARON. I'm not eating / it.

EVA. I don't care. You never eat anything I / make!

AARON. Because you put meat / in it!

CHRISTIAN. Hey, buddy. If you go take a shower, you can keep the turtle.

AARON. Deal. Where's the phone?

EVA. Why?

AARON. I need Dad to pick up crickets on the / way home.

EVA. He doesn't have time for / that!

AARON. I'm not letting Esmerelda starve to death!

> (**AARON**, *box under his arm, grabs the phone and leaves.*)

EVA. Why do you do that?

CHRISTIAN. It makes the kid happy. Why are you up his ass?

EVA. I'm literally graduating high school in an hour. It's the biggest day of my life, and no one cares. You and Aaron are disgusting, Dad's not even here, Mom hasn't bothered to call /

CHRISTIAN. Hey.

EVA. What?

CHRISTIAN. It's okay. Just relax.

EVA. I can't. The chicken will burn.

> (**EVA** *pulls the food from the oven.*)

CHRISTIAN. You look like Mom in that dress.

EVA. It's hers. I went through her closet.

CHRISTIAN. Turn around.

> (**EVA** *twirls.*)

You excited?

EVA. *(Making a joke.)* Everyone's buying stuff for their dorms. I'm looking for a second waitress job to support a turtle.

CHRISTIAN. You should go to college, Eva.

EVA. I will when Mom comes home.

CHRISTIAN. Don't put your life on hold.

EVA. And then what? Dad forgets to wash Aaron's clothes? They live on tuna and noodles?

CHRISTIAN. He's not completely incompetent.

EVA. He's so distracted that he neglects everything. He locks himself in his room and listens to sad music and cries. I mean, we have to leave in half an hour and he's not even home. You can't wear that. You're literally covered in mud.

> (*The phone rings.*)

Aaron, is that Mom?

> (*They wait for an answer. Nothing.*)

CHRISTIAN. I got you something.

EVA. What?

>(**CHRISTIAN** *pulls out a wrapped box.*)

You didn't have to get me anything.

CHRISTIAN. I sorta have a big brother obligation.

>(**EVA** *opens it. A turquoise necklace.*)

EVA. It's beautiful.

CHRISTIAN. Don't tell Angela. She's so freaked out about money with the wedding and the baby...

EVA. You tell Mom yet?

CHRISTIAN. She'll know in two months.

EVA. You have to tell her you're having a baby.

CHRISTIAN. I'll tell her when you tell her you're not going to college.

>(*Touché.*)

>(**CHRISTIAN** *helps* **EVA** *put the necklace on.* **EVA** *wears this necklace through the rest of the play.*)

Hey. I'm really proud of you.

EVA. Thank you. I love you.

>(**AARON**, *unbathed, holding the phone and frozen with shock, enters.*)

Why aren't you in the shower!

AARON. Dad's in prison.

EVA.	**CHRISTIAN**.
What?	What?

AARON. *(Slow and in shock.)* He drove to Nogales this morning to bring Mom home. Bought a refrigerator and tried to hide her in it. He was searched at the border and tried to bribe...a border...patrol...agent.

> *(They stand there frozen. A few still moments, then* **EVA** *grabs the phone, dials. It rings...)*

ANITA'S VOICEMAIL. Hola, este es el telefono de Anita Fuentes Alonso. If this is my babies, eat vegetables and wear clean socks. And no video games before homework! Si es un abogado voy a llamar pronto.

> *(Silence.)*

CHRISTIAN. *(Under his breath.)* That asshole.

AARON. Dad's not an asshole. He was trying to help.

CHRISTIAN. He's a selfish asshole, buddy.

AARON. No, he isn't.

CHRISTIAN. *(Vulnerable.)* He doesn't care about you or me or Eva, okay?

EVA. Stop it, Christian...

CHRISTIAN. *(Gentle.)* Stop what? Telling him the truth? The truth is Billy doesn't care about this family. That's the truth. He's a liar, and the sooner you and Aaron get that, the better.

> *(Pause.)*

EVA. Get in the shower, Aaron. We have to go. I'm not missing my graduation.

AARON. I'm not going anywhere. I'm staying here until Mom comes home.

EVA. She's not coming home, baby.

AARON. How do you know?

EVA. If they caught her, they put her in a detention center.

AARON. *(Resolute.)* No they didn't. She escaped and she's coming home and I'm staying here.

Five

(Hours later.)

(A high school auditorium.)

*(**EVA**, in her graduation cap and gown, stands at a podium taking in the massive crowd of faces.)*

EVA. Hey, class of 2009, how are you guys? Principal Trujillo, looking good in that suit. Mrs. Engles, I'm gonna miss your English class. Rebecca Cleary, you're always gonna be my bff, even when you're halfway across the country.

My name is Eva Alonso. And I am honored to be your valedictorian.

(Reading from her notes.) All school year, I've had a secret dream I've never shared until now. That dream is to have my family here watching me give this speech.

(She looks at all the happy families in the audience.)

So yeah, umm... Sorry, I'm...

(Hands tremble as she fights to keep herself together. Back to her notes.)

As a little girl, I dreamed about falling in love and living happily ever after. And then I grew up and realized a fairy tale was right in front of me. My parents.

When my mom was our age, she tried to cross the border with her baby in July. My dad volunteered for a group that searched the desert for lost migrants. He found them close to death.

He visited the hospital every single day. My mom was too weak to get out of bed, so my dad would bring my brother to her. Rocking him and singing when he cried.

> (**CHRISTIAN** *and* **AARON** *huddle by the phone, waiting for it to ring.*)

Falling in love was inevitable. They got married and tried to get her citizenship, but found out that crossing the border without proper documentation makes it almost impossible.

Still, they refused to give up hope, applying for asylum, visas, everything humanly possible. They tried to keep this a secret from my brothers and me because they wanted us to have a happy childhood where we could dream.

But when I was twelve, my mom was deported. My parents had no choice but to tell us the truth.

> (*The buzz of a jail cell opening.* **BILLY**, *in handcuffs and an orange jumpsuit, enters.*)

We visited my mom in the shelter, but it was too much. She saw how much it hurt us and told us to stop coming.

She was gone for two years, then one night she showed up at our door. Bloody, beaten-up, broken nose, sunburned. She's never talked about what happened. And my brothers and dad and I know never to ask.

Our life went back to normal. Soccer practice, slumber parties, the PTA bake sale my mom organized every year.

My parents' love was unshakeable. Once, I caught them dancing in the kitchen after they thought I'd gone to bed.

Over the summer, my mom was pulled over for a broken taillight. She spent a week in a detention center before being deported to Nogales again. They didn't even bother to let her take a change of clothes.

But every fairy tale has a happy ending. My mom finally got her status adjusted, and was able to come home. She's here watching me graduate, and living happily ever after with my dad...

> (**EVA** *gets choked up. Goes off-script in one messy breath.*)

Actually, that's not true, she's still there, her shelter and our house are exactly seventy-two miles apart. I know this weird random fact because I stare at a map before I go to bed every night, but it might as well be infinite because we don't know if she's ever coming back...

> (*Suddenly embarrassed, she fights to pull herself together. Then goes back to her notes.*)

I share my very personal story because I hope it inspires all of you to live life with open hearts, and be grateful for every moment you get with the people you love.

Today, my friends, we find ourselves thinking only of the future, our dreams, the road ahead and the childhoods we are leaving behind, so I want to leave you all with a quote from William Shakespeare. "It is not in the stars to hold our destiny but in ourselves."

Six

(July. 2010.)

(The kitchen.)

*(**BILLY** is at the stove cooking tuna and noodles. He wears an ankle monitor.)*

(The table is set for two. A burning candle and a dozen roses are in the middle.)

*(**BILLY**'s phone is perched next to him. He's talking to **ANITA**, who we only hear.)*

BILLY. I'm sorry about Blanca.

ANITA. Cats run away.

BILLY. I know, but I liked the idea of you having her curled up next to you at night.

ANITA. I'll get another one. Nogales is full of stray cats having babies.

BILLY. I wish I could put one in a box and mail it to you.

ANITA. Don't do that.

BILLY. I won't.

ANITA. I got the picture you sent.

BILLY. You like it?

ANITA. Aaron's so grown-up.

BILLY. He wants to try out for basketball. I think it'd be good for him. Run all that angst out... That boy's got a deep well. Eva's moving out. She found an apartment with her "roommate," Jay. She says she'll still come by with groceries. I tell her I'm perfectly capable of buying groceries, but she doesn't believe me. It was like herding cats to get everyone together for that photo. Eva can barely get time off. Angela working and the new baby, Christian's so busy with his construction job... He still refuses to talk to me, but he showed up for you... Anyway, I managed to pull it off in time.

(Pause.)

Honey? Are you there?

ANITA. Yes, I... I don't want to talk about the kids tonight.

(Pause.)

BILLY. Okay.

(Pause.)

I decorated the table like our first date.

ANITA. I never had tuna and noodles. You put so much mayonnaise on it!

BILLY. That's what makes it taste good.

ANITA. All I can taste is mayonnaise. And cold peas! It was terrible! The worst meal I ever had.

BILLY. But you ate it all.

ANITA. I didn't want to hurt your feelings. You were muy guapo...

BILLY. I'm still muy guapo.

ANITA. Sí, mi alma...

(Pause.)

BILLY. *(Bittersweet.)* Happy anniversary.

ANITA. Happy anniversary.

BILLY. I wish you were next to me, telling me how terrible this tastes. What are you eating?

ANITA. SpaghettiOs.

BILLY. SpaghettiOs?

ANITA. It was the only pasta I could find. I looked for tuna, but... I put salt on it.

> *(Pause.)*

Sometimes I wish we never had kids. I love them with everything, but I think about a life just us. We'd spend our anniversary in Paris. But then... I feel guilty even thinking it.

BILLY. Don't feel guilty. I think about it, too. I'd have just stayed in Mexico.

(Making a joke.) With you and a new fridge.

ANITA. It was a nice fridge.

BILLY. Oh, well...six more years of probation with an ankle monitor isn't soooo bad... Even if I am a "felon." Officer Garcia thinks maybe I'll get this ankle thing off sooner.

ANITA. I should have never asked you...

BILLY. I'd have tried anyway...

ANITA. Did we make the right choice?

BILLY. I don't know. The kids have lives, a future.

ANITA. Does Christian? I should have taught him Spanish... He'd never survive here.

BILLY. He'll be okay.

> *(Pause.)*

How's your SpaghettiOs?

ANITA. Okay. You?

BILLY. I think I put too much salt in it.

ANITA. You always put too much salt in everything.

BILLY. I know.

ANITA. When I come home, you'll never cook again.

BILLY. There's a new restaurant on Alvernon. They're suppose to have the best guacamole in Arizona. I'm waiting until you come home to eat there.

ANITA. I'll buy a new dress with red high heels.

BILLY. And that lilac perfume...

ANITA. Mmmm... I haven't worn that in years...

BILLY. God, I miss that smell...

　　　　(Pause.)

ANITA. Are you lonely for a woman?

BILLY. I miss you.

ANITA. No, but...feeling a woman... A woman's body.

　　　　(Silence.)

BILLY. Those thoughts come and go. They never last very long. But... It's hard... Are you mad?

ANITA. No. I asked you.

BILLY. Do you have those thoughts? Being with another man?

ANITA. I don't like Mexican men. Too machista. Too much cologne... But sometimes I have those thoughts. Are you mad?

BILLY. No.

ANITA. I miss touch. I miss hands. Rough skin...fingers... I think a person dies inside without touch.

BILLY. Me too.

ANITA. Okay. Now we're making each other sad.

BILLY. I'm not sad. I'm laughing.

(**ANITA** *plays a song in the style of Édith Piaf's "La Vie En Rose" from her phone.**)

ANITA. Get up.

BILLY. What?

ANITA. Up, up!

(**BILLY** *does.*)

We're in Paris. On a bridge with a view of the Eiffel Tower.

BILLY. Okay.

ANITA. Ask me to dance.

BILLY. Would you like to dance?

ANITA. With you?

BILLY. Yes, with me.

ANITA. I don't know, I have to think.

BILLY. You just told me /

ANITA. I won't dance if you complain!

BILLY. Sorry. It would mean everything if I could have this dance.

ANITA. Okay. I'll dance with you. Hold me close.

(**BILLY** *holds the phone to his heart, quietly dancing around the room.*)

---

*A license to produce *72 Miles To Go...* does not include a performance license for "La Vie En Rose." The publisher and author suggest that the licensee contact ASCAP or BMI to ascertain the music publisher and contact such music publisher to license or acquire permission for performance of the song. If a license or permission is unattainable for "La Vie En Rose," the licensee may not use the song in *72 Miles To Go...* but should create an original composition in a similar style or use a similar song in the public domain. For further information, please see the Music and Third-Party Materials Use Note on page iii.

Seven

(December. 2011.)

(The kitchen.)

*(**CHRISTIAN** and **AARON**, sweaty, bound into the kitchen after a game of basketball.)*

*(**CHRISTIAN** cracks open a beer.)*

AARON. You're getting slow, hombre.

CHRISTIAN. I let you win.

AARON. You let me?

CHRISTIAN. I feel sorry for you, going through life with a face like that.

AARON. You know how many cheerleaders I have coming up to me after games?

CHRISTIAN. Liar.

AARON. Okay. I'm lying.

CHRISTIAN. Are you?

AARON. Come to my next game and find out. Oh, that's right. You're busy.

CHRISTIAN. Come on. It's not like that.

AARON. It would be cool if you saw one game before I graduate.

CHRISTIAN. I'll try.

AARON. Sure.

CHRISTIAN. Come on, buddy. We never get to see each other. Don't be like this.

AARON. Like what? I'm having a blast.

*(**AARON** bursts into an impromptu song and dance.)*

"I'M A SEXY SCIENTIST AND I PLAY A LITTLE BALL.
ALL THE LADIES HOLLER WHEN I'M HANGIN' AT THE MALL.
BOOM BOOM SHAKE DA BOOM-BOOM-BOOM!
BOOM BOOM SHAKE DA BOOM-BOOM-BOOM!"

*(**CHRISTIAN** laughs.)*

CHRISTIAN. I just don't like being away from home at night. Too many close calls over the years.

AARON. Okay.

CHRISTIAN. Games go late, and... Angela's SO HORMONAL with her pregnancy. Lisa Marie's been sick.

AARON. But you go to bars.

CHRISTIAN. *(Defensive.)* Bars? No. I don't go to / bars.

AARON. Angela says you go to / bars.

CHRISTIAN. I go to one bar around the corner from our house that I can walk to.

AARON. Okay. So I'll pick you up. I'll drive you home. I'm legal.

CHRISTIAN. Can we not have this conversation?

AARON. Fine.

*(**CHRISTIAN** slams his beer, gets another one.)*

CHRISTIAN. What time does the "master of the house" get back?

AARON. Late.

CHRISTIAN. What time exactly so I don't have to see his lying face?

AARON. Officer Garcia lets him lead a Bible study one evening a month as his "reward" for good behavior.

He usually gets home at midnight. Can you just talk to Dad already? It's getting exhausting.

CHRISTIAN. How's Eva? She still dating Jay /

AARON. Why don't you call her once in a while and find out for yourself.

CHRISTIAN. Fair enough. So...what's up with you, dude?

(**AARON** *shrugs.*)

Any girls you like?

AARON. I'm not really interested in talking about girls.

CHRISTIAN. I'm just trying to make conversation.

AARON. Then ask me what I'm interested in and don't assume it's girls.

CHRISTIAN. You don't like girls?

(**AARON** *flips off* **CHRISTIAN.**)

What are you interested in?

AARON. *(Matter-of-fact.)* Xbox, guitar, and host-parasite interactions.

CHRISTIAN. Host-parasite interactions?

AARON. Yeah.

CHRISTIAN. I don't even... What?

AARON. Like why parasites prefer some species to others, how parasites can be beneficial, and how you stop them when they're destructive. Shit like that.

CHRISTIAN. Cool.

AARON. Yeah, it's pretty dope.

CHRISTIAN. Sounds like it. Dope.

AARON. Super dope.

CHRISTIAN. Yeah.

AARON. Yep.

CHRISTIAN. So that's like what you think about when you're laying in bed at night?

AARON. Yeah, like why does the *Spilopsyllus cuniculi* prefer rabbit blood over, say dogs or cats?

CHRISTIAN. Sure, sure, I often wonder the same thing.

AARON. Why are you asking me questions if you're clearly not interested in talking?

CHRISTIAN. I am interested /

AARON. "Giiiirrrrlllsss."

CHRISTIAN. Sometimes it's nice to live vicariously through other dudes. That's all.

AARON. I bet Angela would loooove that.

CHRISTIAN. You'll understand when you're married.

(*Pause.*)

AARON. I've been thinking about something... And I wanted to tell you before I did anything.

CHRISTIAN. Oh God. Is it porn?

AARON. I'm trying to be serious.

CHRISTIAN. Fine.

AARON. I'm thinking about enlisting in the Marines.

(*Pause.*)

CHRISTIAN. The Marines? Cool.

AARON. Really? You're not mad?

CHRISTIAN. No, no, not at all.

AARON. Because I know how important the Marines is to you.

CHRISTIAN. Yeah, bro, yeah... So you go and enlist and then come back to my place, marry Angela, raise Lisa Marie – you can just take over my life. But we'll have to do some *Face/Off* shit so Angela doesn't get suspicious.

AARON. What?

CHRISTIAN. *Face/Off.* Nick Cage, John Travolta – cut off our faces and switch them.

AARON. Okay... I'm trying to talk to you.

CHRISTIAN. Why?

AARON. I just... Make up for dad fucking up. Prove we're good people. So they won't deport you.

CHRISTIAN. Aaron, I just... Obama's working on the DREAM Act, and if that happens I'll be fine.

AARON. Yeah, okay. They've been talking about that since / forever.

CHRISTIAN. I'll be fine.

AARON. It's not just about you. Angela, you're about to have twins, Lisa Marie, money for Mom so she can move somewhere with a fucking stove! Money for Eva so she can quit one of her shitty bartending jobs and go to school!

CHRISTIAN. But you wanna be a veterinarian.

AARON. Or a zoologist. Or live on a ranch like you did in Iowa. I haven't decided yet.

CHRISTIAN. So do that. You're good at that. You love animals. Who's gonna take care of Esmerelda?

AARON. I thought you could...

CHRISTIAN. Buddy. Hey. I say this with all respect. You're not Marine material. You're scrawny. They'll eat you alive. You won't survive boot camp.

AARON. The recruiter said all that matters is spirit and determination.

CHRISTIAN. You met a recruiter?

> *(Sound of a car pulling up, then a loud wap-wap. Flashing red and blue lights outside the window.)*

> *(**CHRISTIAN** freezes. Eyes wide.)*

> *(Time slows down.)*

(Whisper.) What the fuck...

> *(**AARON** very slowly creeps to the window.)*

Is it Officer Garcia?

> *(**AARON** watches for several tense moments.)*

AARON. No...

> *(**CHRISTIAN**'s heart is racing.)*

CHRISTIAN. Don't make any sudden moves.

> *(**AARON** stands watch at the window while **CHRISTIAN** creeps to the door. Locks it. Turns off the lights. Darkness. Nothing but the flashing lights outside.)*

AARON. Why are they here?

CHRISTIAN. I dunno...

> *(More lights and sirens.)*

What's going on?

AARON. Another car... Are they here for you?

CHRISTIAN. I dunno...

AARON. How would they know you're here?

CHRISTIAN. I dunno...

AARON. Are they gonna deport you?

CHRISTIAN. I dunno...

> (**AARON**, *still looking out the window, starts to panic.*)

AARON. Oh my God oh my God oh my God oh my God / oh my God –

CHRISTIAN. Aaron, you gotta breathe /

AARON. They're getting out of the cars /

CHRISTIAN. Don't let them see you /

> (**AARON** *gets on his knees, still trying to keep watch.*)

> (**CHRISTIAN** *crawls to the table. Getting his keys and wallet.*)

AARON. Oh my God oh my God oh my God oh my God / oh my God –

CHRISTIAN. You gotta breathe, buddy /

AARON. Oh my God oh my God oh my God oh my God / oh my God –

> (*Now police walkie-talkies are heard. Bright flashlights shining through the window.*)

> (*Both* **BOYS** *panic.*)

What do we do?

CHRISTIAN. I dunno... I should go to the church.

AARON. Oh my God oh my God oh my God oh my God / oh my God –

CHRISTIAN. Shhh, you gotta breathe. I'm gonna go to the church. I'm gonna crawl out the window /

AARON. What if they see you /

CHRISTIAN. Don't open the door no matter what they say /

AARON. What if they break down the door /

CHRISTIAN. Shhh, breathe /

AARON. Oh my God oh my God oh my God oh my God / oh my God –

CHRISTIAN. I'm gonna crawl out the back window and walk to the church.

(Getting choked up.) I need you to call Angela. Tell her I love her and Lisa Marie so much... I love you, buddy.

> (**CHRISTIAN** *starts to crawl toward the back. Police walkie-talkies and voices and red and blue flashlights.)*

AARON. No no no no stay here /

CHRISTIAN. It's not safe /

AARON. What if they shoot you /

CHRISTIAN. You're the man of the house /

> (**AARON** *lunges, grabbing* **CHRISTIAN***'s leg.)*

AARON. No no no no no what if they shoot / you –

CHRISTIAN. Aaron, let go /

AARON. No no no no no what if they / shoot you –

CHRISTIAN. Get off me /

AARON. No / no no no no –

CHRISTIAN. Get off me /

> (*They wrestle. Both ad-libbing "let me go" and "no."*)

(While this is happening, the lights and voices disappear. The cars drive away.)

(CHRISTIAN *realizes it first.)*

Wait wait wait shhh...

(They listen. Silent. Dark. Both hyperventilating.)

(After several tense moments, **CHRISTIAN** *creeps to the window.)*

They're gone.

(AARON *bursts into guttural, convulsing sobs.)*

(CHRISTIAN *wraps his arms around him.)*

Shhh... It's okay it's okay it's okay it's okay it's okay...

(CHRISTIAN *rocks* **AARON** *like a baby until he starts to cry.)*

Sorry I'm... I'm sorry...

(They sob until tears turn to hiccups and hiccups turn to quiet.)

We're okay...

AARON. We're okay...

Eight

(December. 2013.)

(Christian's living room. Children's toys and Christmas decor.)

*(**EVA** sits on the couch, drinking hot chocolate spiked with rum. She's buzzed.)*

(Sounds of war are coming from the TV. A news anchor in the background talking about the War in Afghanistan.)

*(**CHRISTIAN**, wearing a homemade cast, enters.)*

CHRISTIAN. *(Absurd.)* I read *The Nightmare Before Christmas* four times... Angela's snoring, but the twins are wide awake saying, "Again, Daddy." How do they not get bored? By round three, all the suspense is gone. We know it's Santa coming down the chimney. How's school?

*(**EVA**, drunk, starts laughing.)*

EVA. *(Buzzed.)* We had to draw blood from each other. I was fine, but Jane, my classmate... When I stuck the needle in her vein, she flinched. There was blood everywhere, and then she passed out.

CHRISTIAN. She passed out?

EVA. She literally turned green and her eyes rolled in the back of her head, and then she's limp on the floor with blood coming out of her arm.

CHRISTIAN. That sounds terrible.

EVA. Nurse Campos comes over, and says give her a second. Jane comes to, and just stares up at us asking what happened. I burst out laughing, which prompted

Nurse Campos to burst out laughing, then Jane starts laughing on the floor – and then she notices the blood and passes out again! Nurse Campos was like, "I don't know if Jane's cut out for this line of work."

> (*They laugh.*)

Is Angela coming back out?

CHRISTIAN. Nope. She'll sleep like a rock.

> (**CHRISTIAN** *tries to crack open a beer.* **EVA** *takes the bottle and does it for him.*)

EVA. You gotta get that set properly.

CHRISTIAN. I'm fine.

EVA. If it doesn't heal / right...

CHRISTIAN. When I get DACA I'll go to a / doctor, okay?

EVA. That could take months. You don't / have months.

CHRISTIAN. Drop it.

EVA. God, you're so stubborn.

CHRISTIAN. I know. Any reports of IED blasts or crazy Taliban suicide bombers on the news?

EVA. Why do you say that?

CHRISTIAN. Say what?

EVA. Seriously?

CHRISTIAN. I like to know if my little brother's alive or not before I go to bed.

> (**EVA** *turns the TV off.*)

I'm sorry. I'm an asshole. Here. This'll make you laugh.

> (**CHRISTIAN** *plays a voice message on speaker.* **AARON** *sounds older, his voice deeper, an arrogance to him.*)

AARON'S VOICE. Yo you sonofabitch. I'm in Kabul. I think you'd like it here. The food is decent. The people are decent. A lot of stray dogs, which is sad, but I'm feeding them every day. Maybe I can bring a few back to the States. Anyway, asshole, happy birrrrthdaaaay!

(A voice of another soldier in the background.)

What? Shut up, butt munch, I'm talking to my brother! It's his birrrrthdaaaay!

*(**AARON** hangs up.)*

EVA. *(Proud.)* He sounds like a prick!

CHRISTIAN. Yep. I knew he had it in him. How's Jay-to-the-ay?

EVA. He asked my ring size.

CHRISTIAN. What? Ahhhhh!!!!!

EVA. Ahhhhh!!!!!

CHRISTIAN. So what are you gonna say?

EVA. *(So in love.)* Yes. He's the best thing that's ever happened to me, like no matter how late I work he always waits up with dinner.

CHRISTIAN. I like Jay.

(A knock at the door.)

*(**CHRISTIAN** and **EVA** startle. They look at each other, unsure what to do.)*

*(**CHRISTIAN** slowly goes to the door. He opens it to find **BILLY**, dressed as Santa and with toys.)*

BILLY. Merry Christmas, ho ho ho.

CHRISTIAN. *(Pissed.)* What the hell, Billy.

BILLY. I'm not Billy, I'm Santa.

CHRISTIAN. Santa comes down the chimney.

BILLY. Yes, but you don't have one so I had to leave my reindeer in a parking garage.

CHRISTIAN. I stopped believing in Santa when I was nine.

BILLY. What do you call a kid who doesn't believe in Santa?

CHRISTIAN. Well-informed.

BILLY. A rebel without a Claus.

>   (**EVA** *laughs.*)

Ho, ho ho! Santa has a present for you. Are you gonna invite me in?

>   (**CHRISTIAN** *stares* **BILLY** *down.*)

EVA. Yes. He is because he's a nice and hospitable gentleman.

>   (*Pause.*)

>   (**CHRISTIAN** *reluctantly motions for* **BILLY** *to enter, but makes it known* **BILLY** *isn't welcome.*)

Officer Garcia know you escaped?

BILLY. He drove me. Gave me till midnight.

CHRISTIAN. You brought your probation officer over here? Why don't you just put a bullseye on my place?

BILLY. Officer Garcia doesn't... His dad isn't legal. He gets it.

CHRISTIAN. You told him?

BILLY. I just... Sometimes he's the only person I have to talk to...

>   (*Pause.*)

I wanted to bring you these...

*(**BILLY** hands **CHRISTIAN** an envelope.)*

All the family stuff for your DACA application. Your mom's never told me much about Mexico... Your biological dad, but that's what I got.

CHRISTIAN. Thanks.

BILLY. Of course.

(Pause.)

I was hoping I could see the girls.

CHRISTIAN. I just got them down, so...

BILLY. I brought them a few things. That doll Lisa Marie wanted... A few books for the twins. And a package from your mom. I'm not trying to disturb your Christmas. I just... I was in that house. Alone... I've never been alone on Christmas.

(Pause.)

I promised you something...and I broke it. I own up to that.

CHRISTIAN. Billy, I...come on.

BILLY. Okay.

CHRISTIAN. I have three kids and a wife. I'm trying to do right by them.

BILLY. So do I, Christian. And I'm trying, too.

EVA. *(Drunk.)* Duuuudes, can we not spiral into the abyss tonight? I put rum in my hot chocolate.

BILLY. I'll go, I just... If we could call your mom. That would mean a lot to her... To think we're spending Christmas together.

CHRISTIAN. Okay.

*(**BILLY** pulls out his phone, dials on speaker.)*

ANITA. Billy?

BILLY. Mi alma, feliz navidad. I'm with Eva and Christian /

ANITA. Feliz navidad, mis amores! I'm so happy you're all together! Where are my grandbabies?

CHRISTIAN. Sleeping. But we'll call you in the morning when they wake up.

ANITA. I only have two minutes. Aaron might call me. I need my minutes.

(*BILLY* cues *EVA and* **CHRISTIAN.**)

(*The family sings a Christmas song together in Spanish, in the style of "Feliz Navidad".**)

---

* A license to produce *72 Miles To Go...* does not include a performance license for "Feliz Navidad." The publisher and author suggest that the licensee contact ASCAP or BMI to ascertain the music publisher and contact such music publisher to license or acquire permission for performance of the song. If a license or permission is unattainable for "Feliz Navidad," the licensee may not use the song in *72 Miles To Go...* but should create an original composition in a similar style, or use a similar song in the public domain. For further information, please see the Music and Third-Party Materials Use Note on page iii.

Nine

(March. 2014.)

(A truck.)

*(**CHRISTIAN** sits in the driver's seat. His cast is gone. **EVA** sits in the passenger's seat.)*

(The sound of a truck engine turning off.)

EVA. Okay, so parallel parking isn't your strongest.

CHRISTIAN. I lined up the mirrors.

EVA. I know, but you slammed on the gas. You have to turn the wheel all the way to the right before backing up. Also, you're never gonna be a NASCAR driver.

CHRISTIAN. What happens if I become a famous NASCAR driver?

EVA. If that happens I get ten percent.

CHRISTIAN. Five.

EVA. I taught you to / drive.

CHRISTIAN. You refreshed / me.

EVA. I don't know what they taught you in Iowa, but it wasn't driving.

CHRISTIAN. They called it "cowboy" driving.

EVA. You've been driving like that without a license?

CHRISTIAN. Nah, Angela stopped letting me drive after Lisa Marie was born.

EVA. Like anywhere?

CHRISTIAN. Yeah. Buses, walking, sometimes I can hitch a ride to work.

*(**CHRISTIAN** rubs his arm.)*

EVA. What?

CHRISTIAN. Nothing. It like...cramps up. Don't say anything.

EVA. Like you should get it looked at because you never got it set and the bone didn't heal right?

CHRISTIAN. Yeah. Exactly. Don't say that.

EVA. *(Anxious.)* We should go. It's getting dark and cops always start lurking in parks when it's dark.

CHRISTIAN. Can we just chill here for a minute?

EVA. Yeah, I just, I'm worried about the cops. When you get DACA we never have to worry about this bullshit again.

(Pause.)

CHRISTIAN. I used to love coming here... Mom and Billy with a picnic. Aaron chasing lizards. We'd eat those devil's food cookies and Mom's tamales and watch the sunset.

EVA. Why did they stop making those cookies?

CHRISTIAN. Lead poisoning.

EVA. I'd stare at the stars and make wishes.

CHRISTIAN. Like what?

EVA. When I was eight I wished for a Spice Girls CD.

CHRISTIAN. I guess we'll never know what they really, really want.

EVA. I know. It's life's greatest tragedy. When I was thirteen I wished for my period.

CHRISTIAN. What?

EVA. I wanted to beat Kristi Lewis and I did. Brought my bloody panties to school to show her.

CHRISTIAN. You're disgusting.

EVA. When I was sixteen I wished for Eddie to feel me up during church.

CHRISTIAN. You're going to Hell.

EVA. I think it was some weird rebellious thing.

CHRISTIAN. Not very ambitious wishes.

EVA. I only told you the ones that came true.

CHRISTIAN. There's still time.

EVA. *(Dark.)* I've accepted that living "happily ever after" isn't in the cards.

CHRISTIAN. Why? What's going on with Jay?

EVA. I gave him the ring back. Told him to move out.

CHRISTIAN. What happened?

> (**EVA** *shrugs.*)

EVA. He deserves better.

CHRISTIAN. No one's better than you.

> (**EVA** *laughs.*)

EVA. The more we talked about the wedding, the more I just... And then I started cheating with these random guys I didn't even like. The whole time I'm thinking about Jay waiting up with dinner.

> *(Beat.)*

Not everyone's capable of what you and Angela have. You're lucky.

CHRISTIAN. *(Guilt.)* She puts up with so much. I don't know why she stays.

EVA. When you get DACA she'll be able to breathe. We all will /

CHRISTIAN. I didn't...get it. I found out a week ago.

*(**EVA**'s stunned.)*

EVA. Are you fucking serious? You did everything right! All the appointments, months of paperwork and fucking biometrics! You're the perfect candidate!

CHRISTIAN. *(Dark and filled with self-hatred.)* I got pulled over in Iowa. Drunk driving. Since the only people slaughterhouses can find are undocumented the judge turns a blind eye. But it happened again. And again. Warrant. So I came home.

(Beat.)

I wish I could go back in time and tell myself there's still hope and happiness.

(Beat.)

Anyway. Now they know. I know they know. There's nothing to run from anymore.

EVA. Does Angela know?

CHRISTIAN. You're the only person I've told.

(They sit there. Listening to the desert.)

EVA. You want an Oreo? I think I have some in my purse.

CHRISTIAN. Yes, please.

*(**EVA** pulls out cookies. They eat.)*

CHRISTIAN. They're not devil's food.

EVA. Not even close.

Ten

(February. 2015.)

(The church.)

*(**CHRISTIAN** sits in a pew staring at his phone. He plays a voice message. It's **AARON**.)*

AARON'S VOICE. Yo you sonofabitch. I'm in Kabul. I think you'd like it here. The food is decent. The people are decent. A lot of stray dogs, which is sad, but I'm feeding them every day. Maybe I can bring a few back to the States. Anyway, asshole, happy birrrrthdaaaay!

(A voice of another soldier in the background.)

What? Shut up, butt munch, I'm talking to my brother! It's his birrrrthdaaaay!

*(**CHRISTIAN** rewinds, plays it again.)*

Anyway, asshole, happy birrrrthdaaaay!

(A voice of another soldier in the background.)

What? Shut up, butt munch, I'm talking to my brother! It's his birrrrthdaaaay!

*(**CHRISTIAN** rewinds, plays it again.)*

What? Shut up, butt munch, I'm talking to my brother! It's his birrrrthdaaaay!

*(**CHRISTIAN** sits quietly for a long time.)*

(Dials.)

ANITA. Mi Rey, I don't have any minutes / left.

CHRISTIAN. You can't talk for a few / minutes?

ANITA. Obama said he's bringing troops home, and now he says he's not since there's a civil war and I need to know if Aaron's okay.

CHRISTIAN. He's okay. He's a pro. Just... We never get to talk.

ANITA. Okay...

CHRISTIAN. How are you?

ANITA. I'm okay...

CHRISTIAN. The girls loved the tamales you sent. They devoured them. Lisa Marie wants cheese and chicken tamales for her birthday. She invited twelve girls to her slumber party so you've got your work cut out.

ANITA. I'll make a hundred. You can freeze them and they'll last the next five birthday parties.

CHRISTIAN. They grow up so fast...

ANITA. Too fast...

> *(Pause.)*

CHRISTIAN. How come you never taught me Spanish?

ANITA. I didn't want people thinking differently of you.

> (**BILLY** *enters with KFC.*)

CHRISTIAN. We've never really talked about any of it. Mexico. My real father...

ANITA. Ay, mijo... So much water...

> *(Pause.)*

> (**CHRISTIAN** *looks at* **BILLY** *as he digests this.*)

CHRISTIAN. Do you think they'll ever let you come home?

ANITA. I don't think so, baby...

CHRISTIAN. How do you live your life without your children?

ANITA. One moment at a time. When I feel sad or angry I thank God for giving my children a better life than I had. And I look at pictures. And my cats.

CHRISTIAN. I wish we'd known each other better while I was growing up... But I was so...

ANITA. We're still here. Still alive. We can know each other better now.

CHRISTIAN. I'd like that.

ANITA. Me too.

CHRISTIAN. Okay, Mom. I'll let you go.

ANITA. Okay, baby. Bye.

> (**CHRISTIAN** *hangs up.*)

BILLY. Hi.

CHRISTIAN. Hi.

BILLY. Hungry?

CHRISTIAN. Yeah. Starving.

BILLY. Good, because I got the "Chicken Feast" and there's no way I can eat it all.

> (**BILLY** *pulls out the food. They eat in silence.*)

CHRISTIAN. Hey... Wanna hear a joke about construction?

BILLY. Sure.

CHRISTIAN. I'm still working on it.

BILLY. Well... I hope you're using a shovel because it's a ground-breaking invention.

CHRISTIAN. I've been thinking a lot about the rotation of Earth. It really makes my day.

BILLY. A furniture store keeps calling me. All I wanted was a one night stand.

CHRISTIAN. I used to work in a shoe recycling shop. It was sole crushing.

BILLY. I've never been to a gun range before, so I decided to give it a shot.

CHRISTIAN. I can't picture you with a gun.

(**BILLY** *waits for the punchline.*)

Oh, that's it. That's the punchline.

BILLY. What? You've really gotta up your game, buddy.

CHRISTIAN. My game is on fire.

BILLY. You've got potential, son – Christian – but you need to study with the master.

(*Silence.*)

CHRISTIAN. Lisa Marie wants this purple bike with pink handlebars. She saw it at Walmart two years ago and hasn't stopped talking about it... I wanted to get it for her, but I just kept thinking... What if she hit her head? What if a car...

BILLY. I know... I know.

(*Pause.*)

CHRISTIAN. They still out there?

(**BILLY** *nods...*)

CHRISTIAN. You call Eva?

BILLY. Yes. And I talked to Mr. Gomez.

CHRISTIAN. And?

BILLY. The longer you run, the harder they'll make it for you.

CHRISTIAN. My girls...

BILLY. I know.

CHRISTIAN. My wife...

BILLY. I know, son... I know.

> (**BILLY** *puts his hand on* **CHRISTIAN***'s shoulder.*)
>
> *(They sit there quietly, lost in private thoughts. Maybe seconds, maybe hours...)*

Eleven

(March. 2016.)

(The kitchen.)

(A "Welcome Home" banner hangs. A few decorations, a cake, and tons of food.)

*(**AARON**, in his service uniform and holding his duffle bag, takes it in.)*

*(**EVA**, in scrubs, and **BILLY** are next to him.)*

*(**AARON** feels like a stranger.)*

AARON. It's good to be home.

BILLY. It's good to have you / home, buddy.

AARON. Oh, man. Frito pie, Cheese Whiz. What! Are those Mom's tamales?

EVA. Yep! Cheese and peppers. It's all vegetarian. They make this vegetarian ground / beef now.

AARON. Oh, man. Thanks, Eva.

EVA. Of course.

BILLY. I made the guac.

EVA. By "make" he means mashing an avocado with a jar of salsa.

AARON. Thanks, Dad. Where are the hot dogs?

EVA. Hot dogs?

AARON. I stopped being a vegetarian in boot camp. It's impossible. MREs are all meat.

EVA. I mean... I could go to the / store.

AARON. No, that's okay. I just really missed gross meat products. I'll go to McDonald's later.

(**AARON** *walks around the room.* **EVA** *and* **BILLY** *are unsure how to respond.*)

BILLY. You looking for something?

AARON. No. I just wanted to make sure nothing's changed. Costco tuna, mayonnaise... Home sweet home.

EVA. Dad's cholesterol is through the roof.

BILLY. It's fine.

EVA. But he refuses to stop eating mayonnaise.

BILLY. It's a staple.

EVA. Don't call me when you have a heart attack.

BILLY. I won't. I'll call 911.

AARON. Let's eat cake.

EVA. It's tres leches.

AARON. Oh shit. Insane.

(**AARON** *cuts a huge piece of cake, dives in.*)

You wanna see something?

(*He pulls out his phone, plays a video.*)

That's my buddy, Jackson. He's from Jacksonville.

EVA. What's he doing?

AARON. Burning shit. Look at his face!

BILLY. This is what you did for fun?

AARON. You think burning shit is fun? It's a job. Oh, you gotta see this guy, Gunther. He pukes.

(**AARON** *plays another video.*)

BILLY. Okay. I've seen enough poop for / one day.

(**AARON** *pushes himself away from the table.*)

AARON. Fine. I won't share my life with you.

>   *(Pause.)*

EVA. ...As much as I want to know everything about your life, I have to go to work / soon.

AARON. I just got here.

EVA. ER's short-staffed. I couldn't get off. I tried.

AARON. Lame.

EVA. I know.

AARON. Call in sick.

EVA. I can't.

AARON. Fine.

EVA. We should call Mom and Christian. I promised we'd call as soon as you got here.

>   *(**EVA** pulls out her phone, dials. On the other end we hear **ANITA** and **CHRISTIAN**.)*
>
>   *(Sadness in **CHRISTIAN**'s voice. World-weary. Lost.)*

Mom /

ANITA. Is Aaron home?

AARON. E4 in the flesh, baby.

CHRISTIAN.	**ANITA.**
Hi, buddy!	Conejito!

AARON. Where's Esmerelda! I can't find her anywhere.

>   *(Awkward pause.)*

Just fucking with you. Eva told me she died and you were too chicken shit to tell me.

CHRISTIAN. Yeah, I... We gave her a funeral. The girls wrote her / a song.

AARON. Cool. How's Mexico. You in a cartel yet.

CHRISTIAN. I'm in three. There's another one that offered me a position, but their benefits package wasn't that great.

AARON. Ah, man. I'm jealous.

CHRISTIAN. So? Back in the Land of the Free. How does it feel?

AARON. Oppressive. Eva won't let me eat meat. Dad hates my shit / videos.

CHRISTIAN. You better not corrupt my daughters with anything gross.

AARON. Don't worry. I will.

ANITA. We're so happy you're home, Conejito. If you need anything /

AARON. You'll drive across the border and bring it to / me?

BILLY. Hey!

AARON. What?

(*Pause.*)

ANITA. So... Your father and I have some news.

BILLY. In two months I'll be a free man. You guys are grown and... You don't need us. I'm going to retire. And then I'm going to go live out the rest of my years in Mexico with my wife.

ANITA. We don't have another lifetime to wait.

(*Silence.*)

EVA. How will you survive?

BILLY. There's a Unitarian church in Nogales. I think maybe I can work with them.

CHRISTIAN. Can you just move here?

BILLY. No. But I am. And if I'm deported... It's my turn to walk across the desert.

EVA. Not with your cholesterol.

ANITA. What's wrong with his cholesterol?

EVA. He's lived off mayonnaise for almost a decade.

ANITA. That will change.

>   (**EVA** *smiles at* **BILLY**.)

We need to do this, babies. And we want your blessing.

>   (*Pause.*)

EVA. Okay.

>   (*Pause.*)

CHRISTIAN. Of course.

>   (*Pause.*)

ANITA. Conejito?

>   (*Pause.*)

AARON. I'm tired as fuck. I can't really... You guys just ambush me with this shit?

>   (**AARON** *hangs up on them.*)

EVA.	**BILLY**.
Hey!	Why'd you do that?

AARON. Do what.

(**AARON** *starts watching cartoons on his phone.* They play through the end of the scene.*)

EVA. Okay... I have to go work... I...wish I could stay. Want me to bring back McDonald's?

AARON. Big Mac. Chicken nuggets. Fries. Apple pie. Coke. Happy meal.

EVA. Okay.

AARON. Chocolate milk.

(*Pause.*)

EVA. Hey.

AARON. What.

EVA. I love you.

(**EVA** *leaves.*)

BILLY. What are you watching?

AARON. *Ren and Stimpy.*

BILLY. Are they... Are they possums?

AARON. Dog and cat.

BILLY. So Ren is, what, the dog or the cat?

AARON. Dog. My buddy Mac was obsessed with this show... I miss those dudes.

BILLY. Maybe you could go visit them.

AARON. Mac got his head blown off by an IED so it'd probably be hard to visit him.

---

*A license to produce *72 Miles To Go...* does not include a performance license for any third-party or copyrighted recordings or images. Licensees must acquire rights for any copyrighted recordings or images or create their own.

BILLY. I'm sorry.

AARON. Don't. Just... Don't say shit like that.

BILLY. Okay.

(**AARON** *goes back to his cake.*)

AARON. *(Matter-of-fact.)* There's all these stray dogs in Kabul. When I first got there, I'd go and buy full meals and give it to them. But then one day, this homeless family comes up to me begging for the food. The dogs are staring at me, this starving woman and her kids. So I gave it to her. These poor skeleton dogs curled up watching this family. I did that for a while. Watching these dogs waste away. And then one day, I just bought a meal. And I ate all of it. And I kept walking. I just kept walking.

Twelve

(May. 2016.)

(The church.)

*(**BILLY** stands at the pulpit.)*

BILLY. If you knew then what you know now, would you still have fallen in love?

> *(Beat as he lets the audience reflect.)*

And then it got me thinking about that verse. "Rejoice and be glad, for your reward is great in Heaven..."

I want everyone to close your eyes, and I'm gonna stand here until you do.

> *(He waits until the audience closes their eyes, then asks each question slow and deliberate, letting the audience picture each image.)*

What does Heaven look like to you? Is it a place? Warm with sand and a big sky? Maybe there's a beautiful sunset?

Are there other people there? Maybe the people you love most? I want you to picture those people, your favorite moments with those people...

Those precious, simple moments...

If you knew then what you know now, would you still have fallen in love?

> *(A moment as he lets the audience digest that.)*

You can open your eyes.

I don't know if there's a literal Heaven, but I do know the greatest reward God can give is love.

We all know love is hard. It asks sacrifice and humility and even heartbreak.

Love is also the most incredible thing we're capable of. It fills us with a sense of purpose and joy even when the world is dark and scary.

What is the meaning of our brief and fleeting lives without it?

> *(The church disappears. We're now in Mexico. The sound of desert wind. Warmth, sand, sky with a beautiful sunset.)*

> *(BILLY and ANITA run to each other. A long and deep and passionate kiss, making up for all the lost years in this single moment...)*

> *(CHRISTIAN and EVA run to each other. They hug.)*

> *(AARON hangs back, watching his family.)*

> *(CHRISTIAN motions to his little brother. AARON hesitates, then runs to him.)*

> *(ANITA runs to her children... Tears, hugs, and laughter.)*

> *(BILLY approaches CHRISTIAN. They look at each other, then CHRISTIAN hugs his father.)*

> *(And then the entire family hugs. Holding each other tight for a very long time.)*

> *(When they finally break, ANITA takes in her daughter.)*

ANITA. Eva, you're a woman.

EVA. I am.

> *(ANITA takes in her baby. It breaks her heart.)*

ANITA. Conejito, you're so grown-up.

AARON. I know, Mom.

ANITA. Oh...

     (**ANITA** *takes in her family.*)

I want you to stay forever.

EVA. I know.

     (*Pause.*)

ANITA. You should get on the road before there's traffic.

EVA. Maybe we could stay for dinner.

ANITA. No, no, it's...unfair. The girls need their daddy.

BILLY. *(Deliberate.)* Remember. When you get to the border, just smile and hand the agent your passports. Don't try to strike up a conversation. Don't offer any information unless they ask.

EVA. I know.

AARON. I'll give them my military ID.

BILLY. Even after you get through the checkpoint, don't stop until you get out of Nogales. But don't speed.

EVA. I know.

BILLY. Once you get out of the city, find a dirt road to pull off on.

ANITA. Make sure you're far enough away from any main roads.

BILLY. Chistian will only have three hours worth of air with the small oxygen tank. People smuggled in car trunks can suffocate and die so make sure you're watching the clock closely.

AARON. We will, Dad.

ANITA. When you go through the checkpoint hold your breath, mi Rey. I think the agents heard me breathing.

CHRISTIAN. Okay.

ANITA. Trust your guts. If something doesn't feel right, stop everything and call us.

EVA. I know.

BILLY. You sure?

CHRISTIAN. If I can tuck my girls into bed tonight... Sleep next to my wife...

>   (**CHRISTIAN** *looks at his mother.*)

El amor no tiene fronteras.

BILLY. You better get on the road before it's dark.

>   (**EVA** *and* **AARON** *start to leave.*)

ANITA. Mi Rey.

>   (**CHRISTIAN** *looks at his mother.*)

I hope I never see you again.

CHRISTIAN. I know, Mom. Me too.

>   (*Trunk slams. Car doors. Engine.*)

>   (**BILLY** *takes* **ANITA**'s *hand as they watch their children disappear.*)

End of Play

www.ingramcontent.com/pod-product-compliance
Lightning Source LLC
Chambersburg PA
CBHW070353120726
47909CB00008B/2834